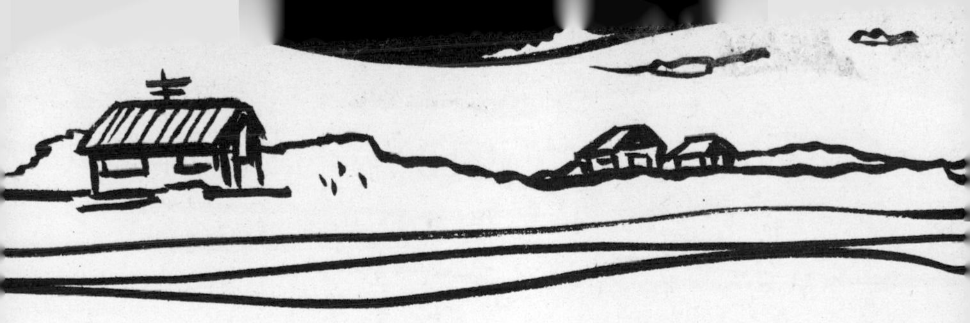

LOST

AT

SEA

# BRYAN LEE O'MALLEY

The people who made it happen:
**James Lucas Jones, Christopher Butcher, Hope, Locke & Studio XD, Jacob & Rey, the band club kids, and my family and friends in London, Ontario, whose lives I frequently plundered for bits and pieces of this story.**

*Book design by* **Bryan Lee O'Malley** *with* **Keith Wood**

*Edited by* **James Lucas Jones**

*Published by* **Oni Press, Inc.**
**Joe Nozemack**, *publisher*
**Jamie S. Rich**, *editor in chief*

ONI PRESS, INC.
1305 SE Martin Luther King Jr. Blvd., Suite A
Portland, OR 97214
USA

www.onipress.com
www.radiomaru.com

Second edition: March 2005
ISBN: 978-1-932664-16-4

7 9 10 8
PRINTED IN U.S.A.

I have a lot on my mind and not a lot to do so it's going to come out, all of it, and then, then, it may begin to make a sort of sense.

It's not like the conversation is stimulating:
Okay. Rules for driving across America, by Ian Taylor.
Technically, we're driving "up" America.

Technically, fuck off!
Please do go on.
I'll take notes, watch.
Okay, one...
Don't drive off a cliff.
No cliffs.
Or into a wall of flame.
I never thought about the wall of flame.
The wall of flame worries me.
OK, next.
Okay, this is on the same note, but—
—don't drive into the GRAND CANYON.
It's easy to do. It's fucking GRAND. It's hard to miss.
Grand... how is that spelled?

Then there's DEATH VALLEY.
Apparently America is full of traps, dude.
Are you listening to any of this?
They can go on for hours...
I'm sorry, what?
Never mind.

The first thing I need to get out of the way is that I have no soul.

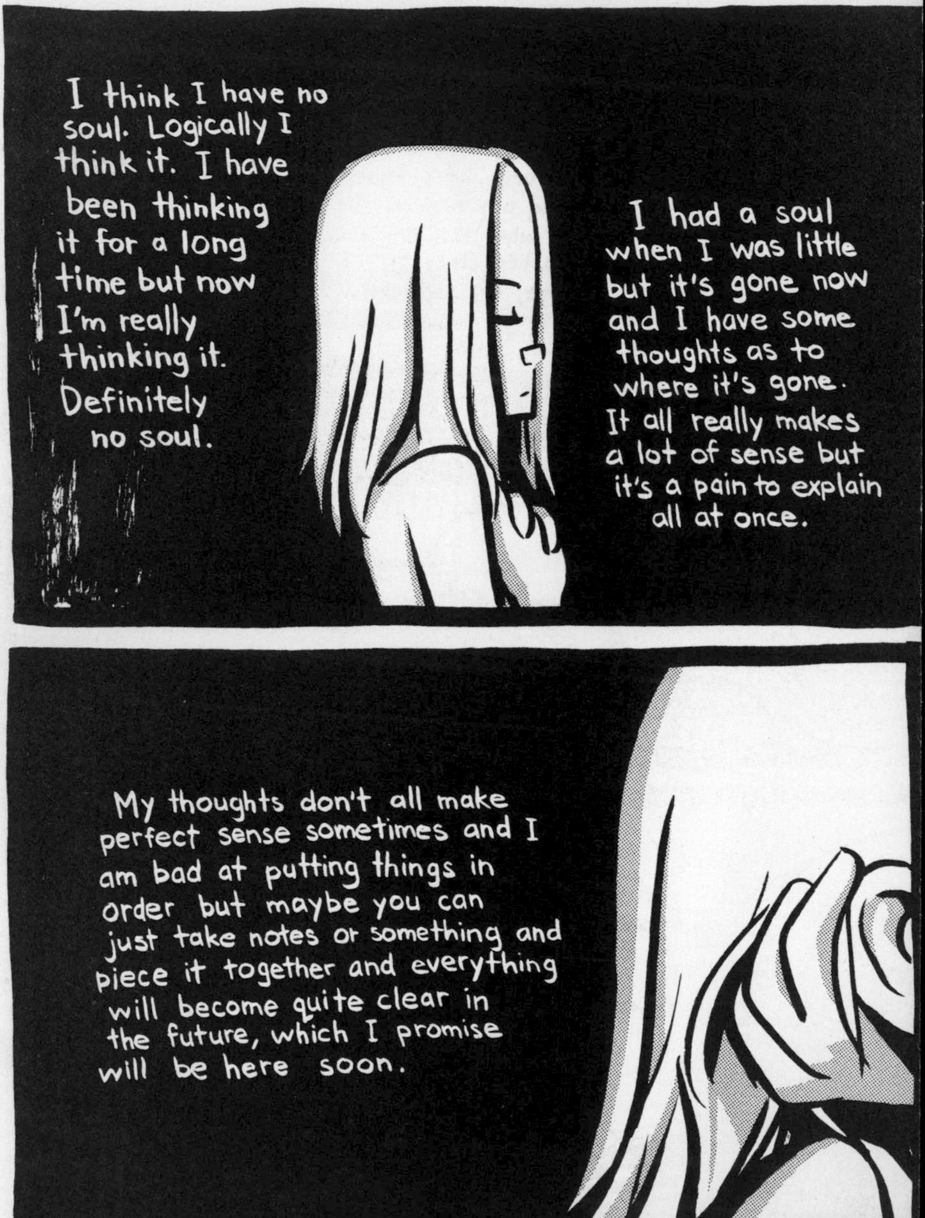

I think I have no soul. Logically I think it. I have been thinking it for a long time but now I'm really thinking it. Definitely no soul.

I had a soul when I was little but it's gone now and I have some thoughts as to where it's gone. It all really makes a lot of sense but it's a pain to explain all at once.

My thoughts don't all make perfect sense sometimes and I am bad at putting things in order but maybe you can just take notes or something and piece it together and everything will become quite clear in the future, which I promise will be here soon.

I don't know what I am writing, what I'm doing. I'm not even writing, I'm only thinking these words, stray thoughts scribbling out to you. I don't know what this is. I don't know. It's a life story. My life story, by me, age eighteen.
The important parts, anyway.
I guess the important parts are what make up the life story and the rest is just the rest.
The rest is just stuff that happens to everyone, like you were born.
And it's not really an important or interesting part of the life story unless it was important and interesting unto itself, like if you were born on a raft on the Amazon or during an eclipse.

But excuse my digressing because I do have a life story and it may not be important or interesting but it begins with a best friend and it ended this morning. Sort of. Well it ends with now, technically, or it doesn't really end at all but it doesn't go past now, yet, at least.
But the last raft on the Amazon part was the part with the boy in California who I have not mentioned,
who I will not mention,
who I dare not mention,
whom I skirt around.

Anyway, I was born.
Does anyone need to stop?
I could smoke soon.
!
Um, I'm okay...
Steph?
Steph's in the zone.

What is this on the radio??
What the fuck is this?!
It sounds like it was recorded in the 1800s!
Dude, it's fucking ELVIS.
What are you, on drugs?
'AIN'T NUTHIN But a hound daaawg
2:49
RADIO
Whatever! Put on a CD! This is totally fucked up!
Dave! CD!!
Shut up. We're stopping.
Look, road stop. We're stopping.
Rest stop
Next exit
Sweet. I think I soiled myself.

This is hard to admit but I am terrified of everything.
Sometimes I get very scared by my own hair falling into my face.
Where I am now, being scared is easiest.
Where is it? A road stop on a highway. California, somewhere, maybe.

And them? We went to the same school. Not here: north, in Canada. True patriot home sweet faraway home. Which is where we're going.
I didn't know them well. Saw them in the halls, not much more. Once Ian and I had to do a presentation together.
MÉTIS
He did all the talking.

I've been on the road with them for maybe two hours, and every minute has been just like this—

Just so you know...
...all my friends are GUYS, okay?
—longer and hotter and smaller and darker and more claustrophobic and so so so much worse in comparison.

In comparison to what? Yes. Okay:

I used to have a best friend.
We did everything together, my
best friend and I.

Things were easier then.
You can sit, y'know.
Smoke?
Oh, um, no, thanks. I don't. Sorry.
SMOKING CAN TOTALLY KILL YOU
SURGEON GEN. WAR.

You don't have to be sorry, Raleigh.
Smoking is fucking stupid. I'm the one who should be sorry, right?
Um...
Anyway, I used to have a best friend.

We met in grade 3; I don't remember how. We were kids. These things happen.

She was always better, faster, stronger than me. She led, and I followed.

I was reticent, easily spooked, short of breath, awful at climbing things.
But look: she tolerated me and I tagged along, I always caught up eventually, and our adventures were marvelous.
I haven't seen her in 4 years, 6 months and 24 days.
?
?
?
?
?
?
?

Dave!
Might I humbly request a smoke?
No. Fuck off.
Yo, light me up, bitch!
Lemme get my CDs out the back, Ian!

Yes, she is always like this.
Shit!
Uh, Raleigh?
I think your bag ripped.
I'm really sorry.
It must have caught on some-thing.
I think I have a garbage bag you can use for now...

So anyway

I had this dream. It felt like I'd had it before, or been in that place before, but maybe I just dreamed that I dreamed, or... or something. Anyway, it felt huge. Ominous and unsettling and familiar. The details were as follows:

There were cats?
NO
Definitely the word "NO".
Vague uneasiness?

When I woke up in someone else's faraway bed ten thousand years ago, this morning, it was so clear. I close my eyes. I try to remember.
They think I'm asleep. Wouldn't that be nice? Some people must fall asleep really easily.
Did you ever talk to her in school?
Who, Raleigh? No.

We did a thing on Louis Riel in Knoch's class.
She was... quiet.
She always struck me as one of those people who's really... self-contained. faraway.
One of THOSE people, eh?
Cool on her own terms.
She's pretty cool.
She's pretty weird.

Cold, grey, useless Sturton Academy.

I knew them, or of them. Stephanie Ferguson, Ian Taylor.
Dave Weldon— wasn't he going out with what's her name, like, forever?
They were part of a larger group of friends.
I want to say I had no friends

but, I mean,
that's bullshit.
I had cold, grey,
useless friends
to match
everything
else.

What should we get on it?
Meat!
Vickie's PIZZA
Raleigh?
Um...
I kind of, um, don't eat meat.
Girls, man...
Awww, Davey.
Um, what?
SHE was vege-tarian.
Yeah, and so's Steph, so what the fuck do you guys want?
Double cheese and mushrooms, man.
Um, yeah, sounds good.

...half mushroom.
Vickie's
"She?"
Dave's ex, M-
Stephanie.
So ANYWAY.
I think we're making good time.
Good time? Where the hell are we?
I dunno. Northern California.
Weren't we in San Francisco, like, this morning?
Yeah.
Isn't THAT northern California?
I guess...
You in some big fucking hurry to get home, now?
Ehh. Point.

After the past week
I'm ready for anything.
I'm ready for anything.
WANDER INN
VACANCY
Is Ian still in the bathroom?
Yeah. ...How long has he been in there?
Like fifty million hours.
I got ice.
Dave's having another smoke.
You don't mind if I change, do you?
Um...
No...
Ian's such a girl.
Honestly. I could tell you stories.

He makes me feel so manly.
Um, you dropped a flower.
Oh, thanks.
What are you reading?
Oh..."Harry Potter à l'école des sorciers"
I like how that's studious and yet totally not.
Do you have a brush?
brush brush
brush brush
I'm looking at that bed, and you know what I see?
Um...
...not... a bed?

TRAMPOLINE!
Woo! Woo! Woo!
Aww yeah!
C'mon, Raleigh
Don't look at me like that

I think you should totally
be bouncing also
hee hee
hee hee

aaa
aaaa
aaa

aaa
aa
aaa
aaaa
aaaa
aa
I dream of
a zillion cats.
meow
meow
meow
meow
meow

It was something like December of grade 8. The parents were weird. The home situation was falling to bits. At school, my best friend said:
I'm moving.
What? Where??
To Ottawa.
What??
For my dad's work.
And she did.

The following summer is when they got my soul.
I mean, I think.

meow
meow
meow
meow
meow
?

Morning.
Smoke? I stole Dave's.
No, thanks. Um, I don't smoke.
Ever tried?
Uh... no.
You're a better man than I.

Your dress is really pretty.
Thanks.
I got it at Value Village for $3.
Um...
Why were you meowing earlier?
?
What? M— I was meowing?
Yeah. Well, I think so.
WANDER INN
VACANCY
I'm sure there was a good reason, then.

I didn't mention how hard it was to stand up
and brush my teeth
and breathe
but somehow, it's better in the morning.
Honest.

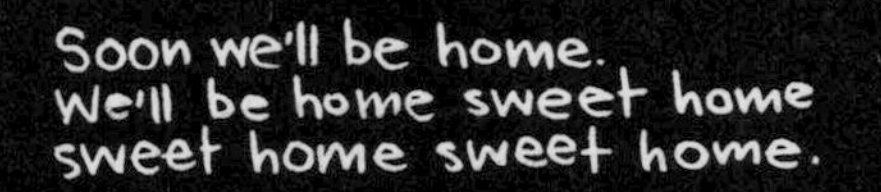
Soon we'll be home.
We'll be home sweet home
sweet home sweet home.
And now I want
to cry again.

Turn this shit up, yo!
IT IS ALGERIA AND MY CITY IS ORAN

My first name is Amal and I'm a girl, I'm a girl, la la!!!

Now I'm laughing.

GOLDEN ANGEL
DINER
Booths totally rock!!
FLES STEAKS
PANCAKES
GOLDEN ANGEL
CHICKEN
I concur.
Incidentally, I'm fucking starving.
I gotta pee. Move over.
Hang on...
Oh, hey, wow.
Dude, that was fast.

You said "dude."
SHIT!
Uh... I mean... yeah... no.
I totally didn't swear?
Didn't hear a thing.
Uhh... y'all have a bathroom?
Just back thataway on your left, dear.
You kids enjoy, now.
I'm sure we will.

"Y'all?"
How'd Ian get so full of shit?
Surgery?
Superior breeding, I think.
Would you care to say grace, Steph?
Shut the fuck up.
Food sounds really great until I see it in front of me.

I guess it's not possible to just stop eating, right?
Maybe I'll waste away. That would be very literary.

You want me to tell you why I'm here, in this insane car with these insane people. I want to tell you, too. I'm practically bursting. But we're not ready yet.
PORK
55
It's just, it's such a long story. It's so long and it's not at all straight in my head. Nothing really is at this point.
MOVERS
TISH COLUMBIA

I told you about the beginning. What happened next was mom and dad split. Mom got me and we moved to the new house and dad took off and mom got a great job and I got to go to Sturton.
And I ignored my boring friends and lost most of them and in grade eleven Mr. Santiago suggested that I visit a writing forum on the Internet and that changed every-thing.
and that was where I met him:

You
Him
Stillman
Your name is Stillman.

When I was with you, I was perfect.

I was never good at being with people.
I never really figured it out

until I met you

and then it was easy. I didn't have to try, because it all came naturally and everything was so right.
Was it the same for you?

Now I talk to you as if you're here, but you're not, he's not, I'm just talking to myself again.

In grade three they took me out of class and told me I was gifted. I think it surprised them as much as me.
They told me everyone else in the gifted class they hastily threw together wasn't "really" gifted.
Aa Bb Cc Dd Ee Ff Gg H
They were just there to make me feel comfortable.
Sometimes I wonder if they told all those kids the exact same thing.
No. 2 PENCIL
No. 2 PENCIL
It was a tiny school and I liked it and, yeah, gifted class was probably my favourite.
I have to assume it totally fucked me up.
Raleigh?

Blondes really actually do have more fun, right?
Um... some of them?
No, no, Raleigh's okay.
I'm talking about, like, blonde eyelashes.
Those are a little, how you say, "gauche."
Same with like, really pale red-heads.
Redheads are trolls.
I dunno. I could be coerced into dating the right redhead.

You know, like, Wendy's?"
That chick. Wendy. I'd do her.
Oh yeah?
I could totally go for some Wendy's.
STU's
CHARBROILED FOODS
This is not Wendy's.
Oh, come on.

You don't even LIKE Wendy's.
Yeah, and I fucking love THIS hole.
Sometimes it's good to give your money to someone other than "the man."
HA Ha HA hee HA
HA ho HA HaHA HA ha ha HA HaHA Ha
Ha
ha HA Ha Ha ha hee
hee hee hoho HA ha ha ha
Anytime I do something that isn't totally embarassing, I feel like such a faker.

I get thoughts like:
I look in the mirror and I don't belong there. I see myself and I look all wrong. Stephanie looks bold and bouncy and fresh and normal, and I look like something else. Too long, too stringy, too pasty, too squarish, kind of inhuman.
What is it that makes me not fit in, and is it in the world, or in my head? Why do I look like a mutant in photographs, anyway?

Man, I wish I was tall.
I always kind of hated it, actually.
Really?
But you always seem so sure of yourself.
I do?
And you don't slouch, like a lot of tall girls.
Umm... my mom always told me to stand up straight!

*sigh*
I'll have to settle for "cute."
Smek
I'll never be beautiful like you and your hideously perfect kind.
Anyway, of course you hate being tall.
That's how it works, Raleigh.

Can I look at your cell phone?
Um...I guess?
It doesn't do anything cool, though.
Careful. Last time she touched a cell phone, we ended up with YOU in the car.
Only because you keep every number in your phone that you ever dialed even once for homework, stalker boy!
More like because you're technologically retarded!

You called me by accident?
Well, not exactly, but—
bi bi bi bi bi
—aa aaa!!
bi bi bi bi bi bi
b bi bi bi bi bi
...Hello?
Hey, where are you?
Are you getting in tonight, or what?

Um, no. I'm in a car. I'm getting a ride in a car.
Whose car?
Um, some kids from Sturton.
You met up with Sturton kids in California?
I know, what are the odds, right?
So are they pompous-ass rich kids?
Jesus, mom.
Um, they're nice. We're friends. They're okay.
Well, okay, well, that's good. How was your father?

My father, I forgot to mention this, but my father lives in Fremont now— that's near San Francisco, that's in the Bay Area or whatever. He has a job that I don't know a thing about and he lives with a woman who has dark hair and no personality and served me chai tea.
He still with that woman?
Um, fine.
Yeah.
My dad, his character arc is that he was here and then he left. He was a nice dad, but maybe not a great husband? There were infidelities. There have been other women. My mom, she's been single since, you know, then.
My poetic job description for him is "emotional hobo." This has something to do with hitching metaphorical trains.
Carla?
Krysta.

I saw him the other day and he said, and this is the only thing that stuck in my mind:
Your mother doesn't know what love is, Raleigh.
I think I'm getting roaming charges or whatever.

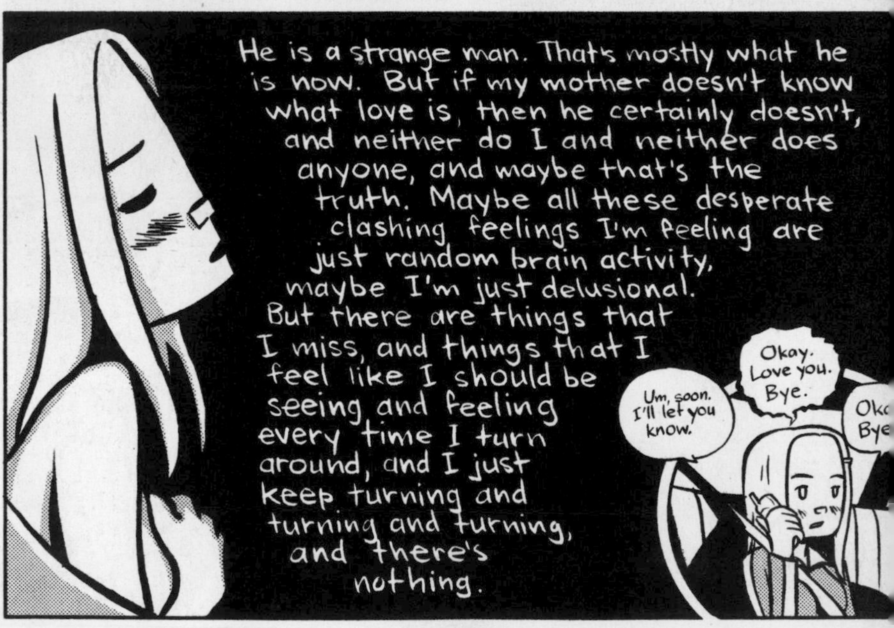
He is a strange man. That's mostly what he is now. But if my mother doesn't know what love is, then he certainly doesn't, and neither do I and neither does anyone, and maybe that's the truth. Maybe all these desperate clashing feelings I'm feeling are just random brain activity, maybe I'm just delusional. But there are things that I miss, and things that I feel like I should be seeing and feeling every time I turn around, and I just keep turning and turning and turning, and there's nothing.
Um, soon. I'll let you know.
Okay. Love you. Bye.
Bye

Hey, what— what direction are we going?
I can't make out the compass.
Uhh... north-west.
More like west.
Kind of more like southwest, actually.
South, actually. Totally south.
You FUCKS! I KNEW it!!

Um, yeah, no, see, we're— we're stopping for the night!

Will we EVER get home?

YOU could drive if you had a licens slack-ass.

So when do I get to drive?

You okay? You look a little peaked.
Uhhhhh...
Yeah. Just tired?

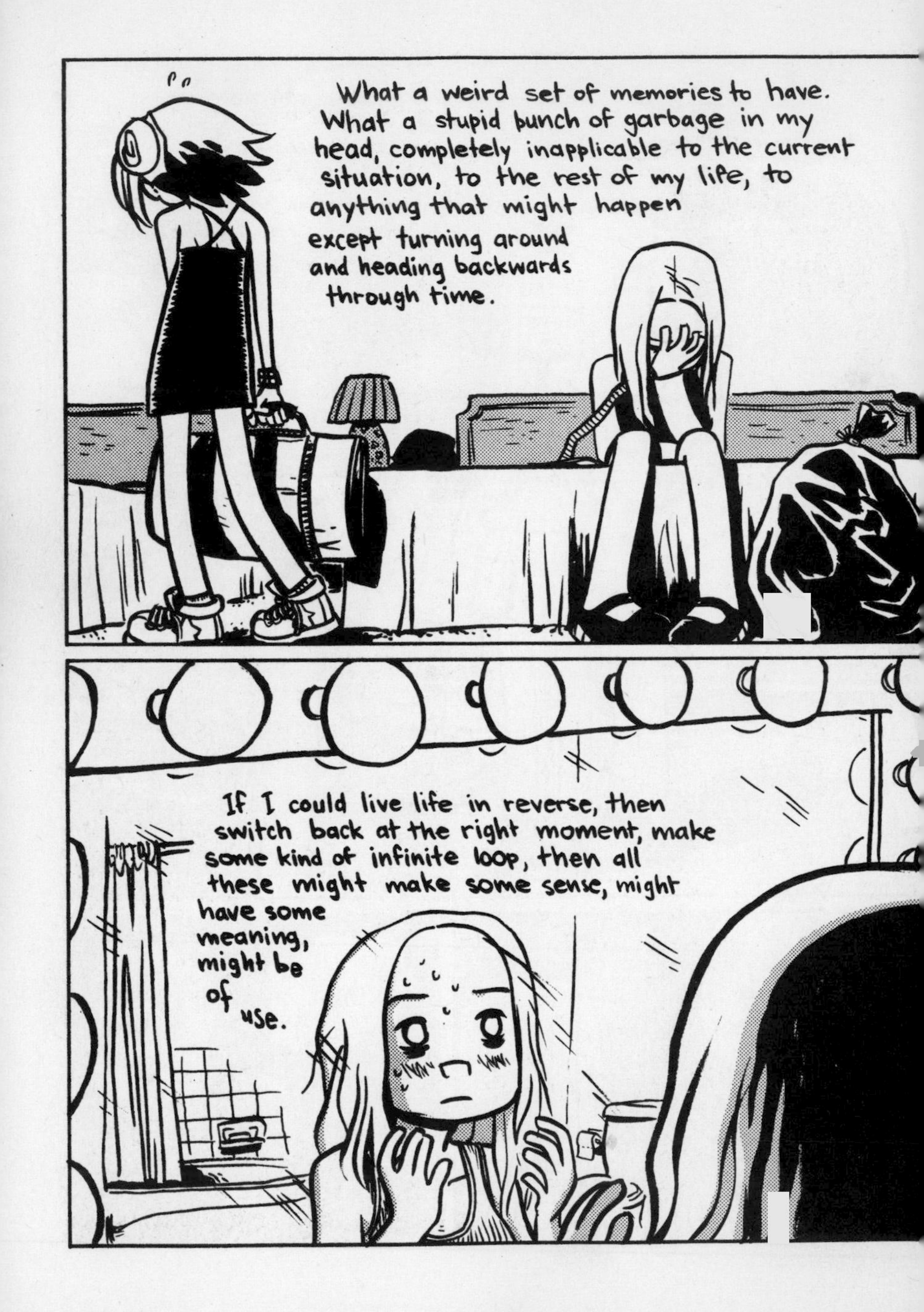
What a weird set of memories to have. What a stupid bunch of garbage in my head, completely inapplicable to the current situation, to the rest of my life, to anything that might happen
except turning around and heading backwards through time.
If I could live life in reverse, then switch back at the right moment, make some kind of infinite loop, then all these might make some sense, might
have some meaning, might be of use.

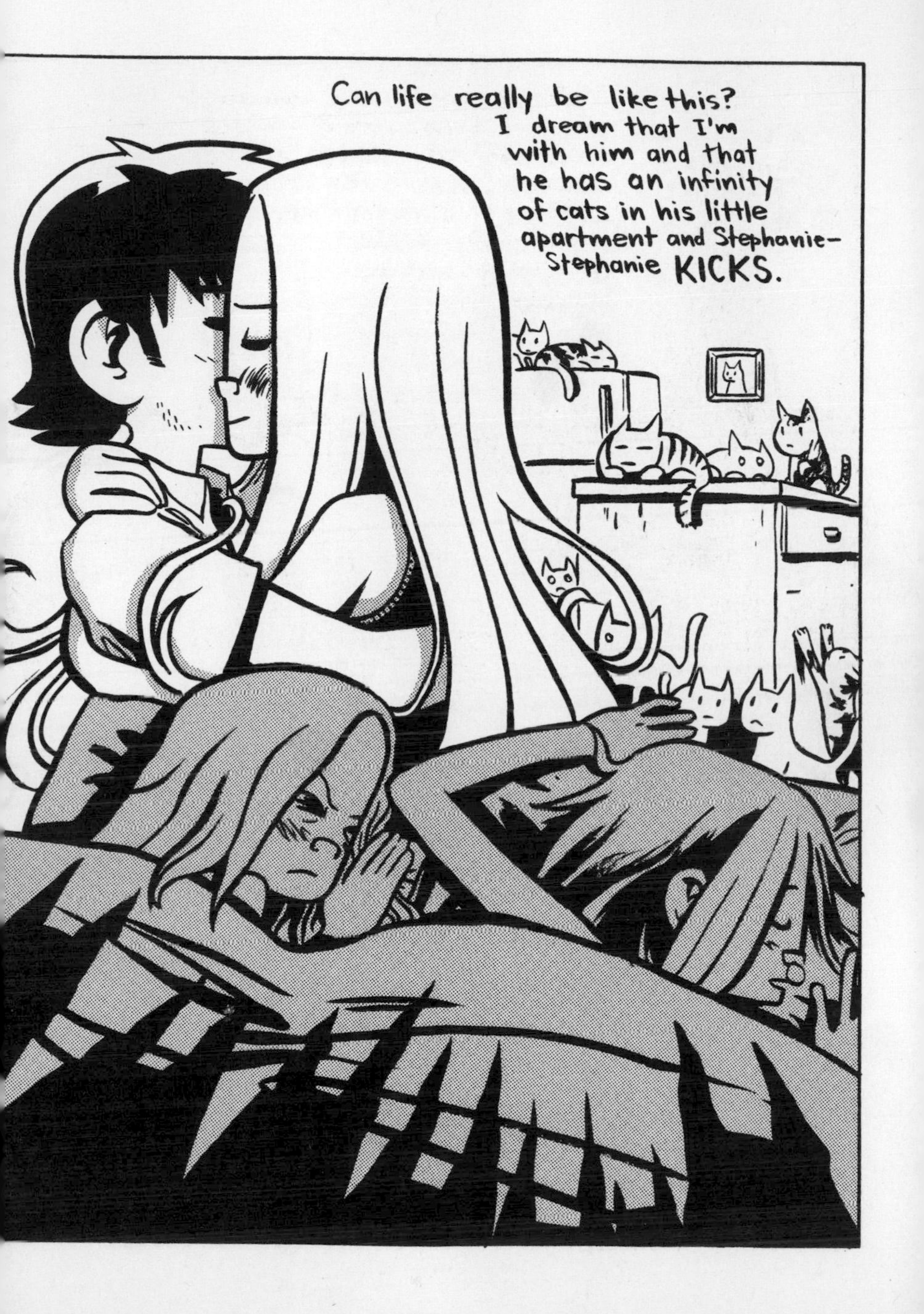
Can life really be like this?
I dream that I'm with him and that he has an infinity of cats in his little apartment and Stephanie-Stephanie KICKS.

Stephanie kicks me entirely awake and keeps me there. And I just keep thinking of cats, feeling surrounded by cats. Cats cats cats. Why cats? Why do I keep seeing cats? I'm allergic. I have very little experience with them. It doesn't make sense.

I lie awake. I think of cats. I think of Aunt Helen and her giant fuzzball under the bed, hissing and taking swipes at l'il Raleigh, age 6. We couldn't stay the night because my eyes wouldn't stop watering, my breath stopped coming.
I had a scar on my arm my entire life and then, this year, I looked at that spot and realized it was gone.
No more scar. Just a memory.

My best friend had a cat. Samantha—Sam. The only cat I wasn't allergic to. White, short-haired, bored, uninterested in our little boy activities.
z
Carrie from high school had a cat, too. Black and white, hairier than Sam, I couldn't sleep over at the sleepover. We did each other's hair and makeup, for serious. My mascara ran.

Cats, cats, cats.
Fucking cats.
Ugh...
What time is it?
Like 10:30.
Get the fuck up, Ian.
C'mon!
Muh...
smack.
C... continental breakfast...

Um...
I have this problem.
Is it gross or personal?
I'm really no good with either gross or personal.
No, I- I see cats.

You see cats.
nod nod nod nod
Seriously? Do you see any right now?
Straight ahead.
He just went into the tall grass, see?
Hmm...
Oh, hey, I see him!

So is this like, really weird for you?
It's not like—it's just—
...It keeps happening. Cats everywhere.
Like my eyes are irresistibly drawn to them.
I can't make it stop.
Well... I mean... how about you show me every cat you see today?
Maybe if we both see 'em, it'll mean you're not crazy.
Maybe. Maybe I—
What?
8
Nothing. Brain fart. I'm just confused.

I'm just confused. Everything's confusing. Everything beautiful is far away, or maybe everything far away is beautiful. It's like how the grass is greener on the other side. Grass just looks nicer from the other side, you know? Grass where you're standing looks like dirt with green hair.
Rest Area
5 MILES
Right now I miss home and I miss my mom and my books and my Mac and my Stillman. The only thing I don't miss is this car and these kids. Is it weird that we only miss things when they're gone, or is that inherent in the meaning of the word?

I wish I had my dictionary.
?
rub rub
Now they're coming right up to me. This is bullshit.

Heyyy...
See? Cats.
Not crazy.

SHOO! SHOO!
That's a fabulous dress, Raleigh.
Shoo! Fuck off!
Oh... thanks.
This is my favourite dress. The thought of wearing this dress is all that got me out of bed this morning. I haven't worn it since... god... yeah.

Are we going?
Uh... yeah.
Are you, like, okay?
Yeah...
No.
Maybe.
I'm... I'm getting there?

Time is funny today. Everything's kind of fucked. I think Dave and Ian maybe had breakfast at the motel, but Stephanie just smoked, and I just watched. Hours are slipping by in this kind of fugue state. My thoughts are sludge, and now all my favourite dress is doing is bringing back memories of you. Him.
Whatever.
Something else, something else... I got this dress for the graduation dinner my mom held supposedly for me. She throws dinner parties for scary expensive people. I guess you could call her a socialite?
Some of her people are pretty famous and important. I think she knows that one guy. Yeah.
Okay. I forget.

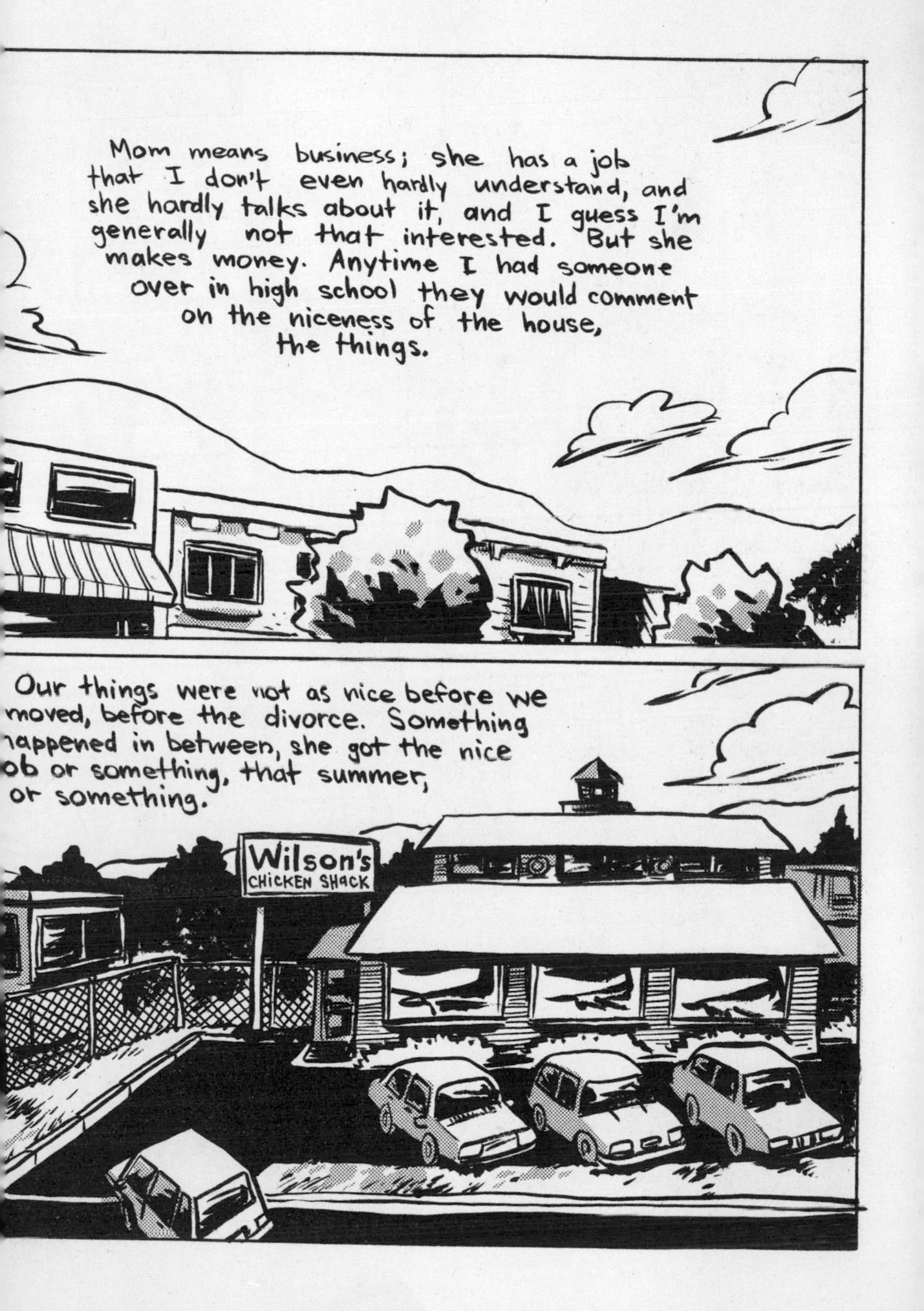
Mom means business; she has a job that I don't even hardly understand, and she hardly talks about it, and I guess I'm generally not that interested. But she makes money. Anytime I had someone over in high school they would comment on the niceness of the house, the things.
Our things were not as nice before we moved, before the divorce. Something happened in between, she got the nice job or something, that summer, or something.
Wilson's
CHICKEN SHACK

Four, please.
It'll just be a minute, okay?
No problem, man.
Oh dude, they have all these photos on the wall of all the crazy people who ate here or whatever.
This is pretty gruesome.
People scare the living shit out of me
Huh... this girl looks like you, Raleigh.
What? Where?

That's weird...
Do you have sisters?
No...
Have you ever, like... been around here?
That's kind of creepy, man...

Thank you, fried chicken. *BURP*
Can we maybe just sit here for a while and digest?
vrrrt vrrrrt
turn
vrrrt vrrrt

TURN!
vrrrrrrrt
rrt
I was just kidding?
vrrrt
rrt
vrrrrrrrt
vrrrrrrrt

So?
What's the deal?

Do you girls even have any idea what goes on under the hood of a car?
SLAM!
Just shut up.
!
I guess we should have studied harder in that class on how to be men.
Maybe you can catch up in university.
HA HA Ha Ha ha ha H ha HA HA Heehee hoho

This is bullshit.
J. HAWKES AUTO
CLOSED
CLOSED
I think they're closed.
This is such bullshit.

Well, it's Sunday.
Yeah, man. Let's just stay in town for the night.
We'll get them to look at the car in the morning or something.
Fuck you fucks and the fucks you fucked in on!
Yeah. Sure. Uh-huh. What-ever.
Let's go. Let's just fucking go.
Go WHERE?
Quit yer goddamn hee-hawin' and let's skedaddle.
WHAT?

Do you believe in fate? Do I believe in fate? Would fate put me in the same places again and again, putting all the pieces of the puzzle right in front of my nose? Is there even a puzzle? Why do I keep asking questions and not answering any of them? Where the hell are we? Are we still in California?

Are we still in California?
CLEA
CLOSED

I think we're in Oregon.
Um...
*
Do you even KNOW?
DAVE is the navi-gator!
I wasn't just paying attention.
I was just driving aimlessly, as per usual!

I apologize for this on behalf of Ian.
Um... it's okay. Really.
Like it's my fault, asshole!!!
Oh no.
I've... gone... too... far.
JACK'S
Boucher Boutique
CLOSED
DARKS
closed
Ian sucks, man.
I know it.
What kind of town shuts down by 4 PM on a Sunday, anyway?

This store looks so cool.
They have these weird cat pillow thingies.
What? Like, pillows for cats?
Mona Lee Kitty's
CLOSED
They're sort of cat-shaped pillows.
I think they have, like, hand-embroider faces or something.
Mona Lee Kitty's
This fucking sucks.

This doesn't bother me, the waiting.
The meandering. The not getting anywhere. Life is like that, right? When we were little, my best friend and I would always go down the paths we hadn't been down before, even if they usually went nowhere— even if we didn't know where we were. Road trips with my dad behind the wheel— yeah. You can imagine. Aimlessness has been a way of life.

This specific trip, even,
California to home: this isn't the first time I've taken it. This [illegible] is a recurring theme for me. I'm sure it means some[illegible]g, but I'm kind of bad at taking meaning from things that way. The cats, the road, mom, California, Vancouver and everything in between. It means something to have no soul and no friends and [illegible]oo many cats that I can't even [illegible]ouch. What does it mean?

That summer when I was 14, after my best friend left, after my dad left; the summer before high school. I think I still had my soul, because I don't remember being a horrible person. Mom put me in the car and we drove down to Modesto, CA, to Aunt Lynette's. She takes care of foster kids and she took care of us, too, until mom said she was ready to go face the world again.
ZZZ
And then we drove back. The same trip. The same route. The route of not knowing or caring when you'll get home, just sort of assuming you'll get there eventually. Maybe we even stopped in this town. California. Somewhere. Maybe Oregon. And mom had a new purpose, a new drive, and things got better for her. She put things behind her.
SNOW WHITE inn
VACANCY
This place is pretty sketchy, eh?

In a good way, though, right?
OFFICE
No...
OFFICE
Hey... Cat.
SNOW WHITE inn
VACANCY
Seen it.
SNOW WHITE inn
VACANCY

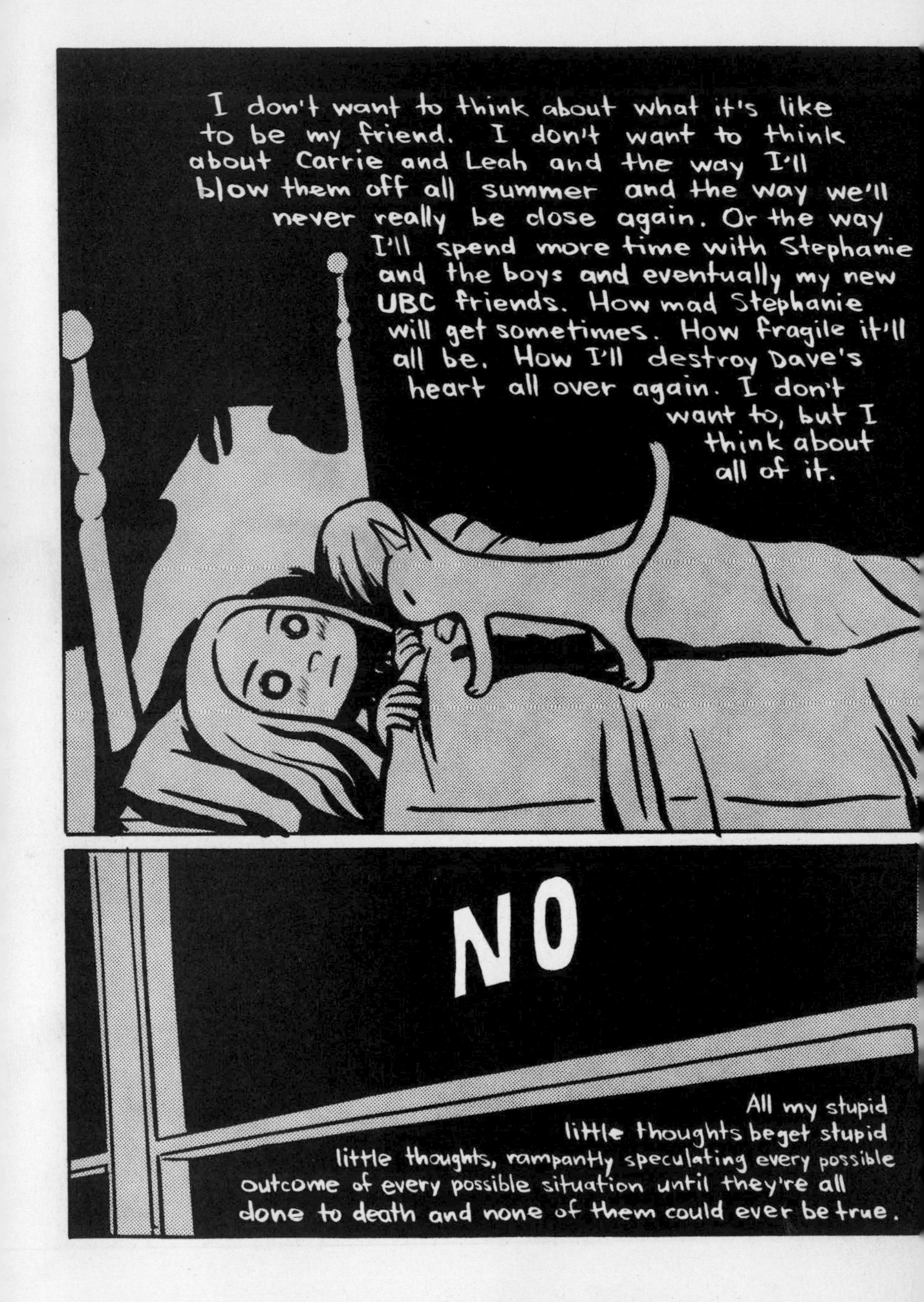
I don't want to think about what it's like to be my friend. I don't want to think about Carrie and Leah and the way I'll blow them off all summer and the way we'll never really be close again. Or the way I'll spend more time with Stephanie and the boys and eventually my new UBC friends. How mad Stephanie will get sometimes. How fragile it'll all be. How I'll destroy Dave's heart all over again. I don't want to, but I think about all of it.
NO
All my stupid little thoughts beget stupid little thoughts, rampantly speculating every possible outcome of every possible situation until they're all done to death and none of them could ever be true.

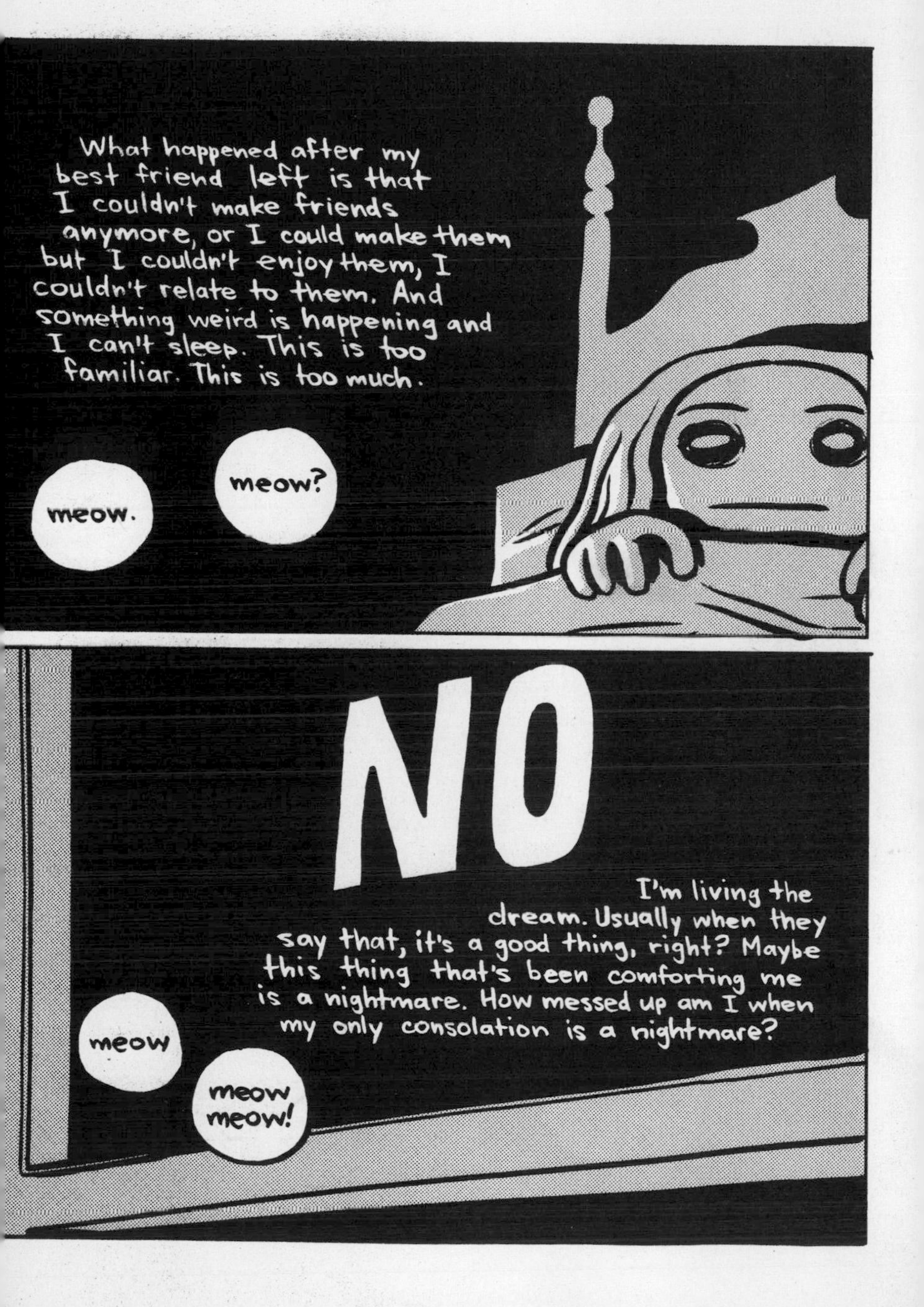
What happened after my best friend left is that I couldn't make friends anymore, or I could make them but I couldn't enjoy them, I couldn't relate to them. And something weird is happening and I can't sleep. This is too familiar. This is too much.
meow.
meow?
NO
I'm living the dream. Usually when they say that, it's a good thing, right? Maybe this thing that's been comforting me is a nightmare. How messed up am I when my only consolation is a nightmare?
meow
meow meow!

NO
Fuck fuck fuck fuck fuck fuck fuck fuck.
meow!
meow, meow!
NO
Fuck.
meow meow!?
meow??
meow meow meow?

BAR & GRILL
meow
meow?
Fuck you! Leave me alone!!

My heart is pounding. My mind is racing. My imagination is working overtime. So what if I have no soul? What if there was a bad man in the hotel bar, what if my business-minded mom saw a way to get what she wanted? What if the cats mean something? What if everything is evidence? What if it all makes so much sense?

SNOW WHITE inn

oh, god...
There you are.
Are you going back to bed?
I was gonna smoke this bitch.
Stephanie-

I've never thought of myself as a talker

but
sometimes...

I have to tell you something.
What?
I have to tell you that I have n soul.
Oh my god, are you a vampire?
No, I'm–
I'm huma with no soul.

Were you born that way?
No. I think-
I think my mom sold it when I was 14.
To the devil?
Yeah, the devil or something. In a hotel bar.
At the Snow White Inn. This is the place.
This place here?
Yes! I have these—these dreams. With the "NO," you know? And the cats.
She met him in the bar, they went back to the hotel room and she, she gave him my soul.
There were a million cats.

Wait, why? Why'd she sell your soul?
What'd she get?
She... she traded it for her success.
I think. I mean, sh successful
She's got this amazing job and she's practically a millionaire now and she got me into Sturton just like that.
And... and cats.
And sisters! I think— you know, you remember, that photo in the restaurant? SISTERS!
Two of them, and the devil took them!
And... and... and so many cats. And he put my soul in a cat and watched it run away?
And... and maybe my sisters are cats too?
I— I don't know.
I'm tryin to figure it all out.

Silence. What's she thinking?
Am I insane?
Am I retarded?
Cats, eh?
Uh... yeah.
I mean, I guess my soul is in a cat.
Somewhere in this town, or something.
So why don't we go find it?
...What?

Z Z
CLICK
Hey, wake up.
We have to go find Raleigh's soul, it's in a cat.
So... wait... what are we doing?
We're hunting cats to get Raleigh's soul back.
Oh.

How do we know which cat has your soul?
Um... I was thinking if I looked in their eyes and tried to penetrate deep within, I could like, see their souls?
And like... if it's the right one, it'll like automatically transfer over when in such close promixity to its true owner, or something.
Okay, cool.
No cats yet. Maybe we should fan out a bit?
You guys go on...

You cold?
Sorta... it's chilly. I didn't realize earlier.
TORONTO
I'm glad I stole Ian's sweat-shirt.
Here, wear this.
It'll give you inner strength.
Uh, okay...
TORO
Oh, shit-
NTO

cat!
NOD!
Hiiii,
kitty...

Here, kitty kitty, or some-thing.
Hey kitty. Nice kitty.
QUICK! Do the eye-staring thing!
MIAAA!?
Oh my god, this is so deranged.
meow wwww
Just do it!
---

I...
No?
I don't... feel anything.
Good enough!
Holy shit!
ZOOM

We already checked that one! Ignore it!
Wait! Raleigh, c'mere!
TORONTO
I'll keep looking, okay?
Okay...
Hi.
Dude.
I got my own, and it's not terribly happy.
Check it.
?
Whoa! Watch it...
Shit!

Not yours?
I guess not...
TORONTO
Buck up, l'il cowgirl! We'll find your soul!
BIG
TORONTO
There's another one! They're everywhere, man!
I TOLD you!
mew?
Oh!

meow?
URF
Just like the good old days.
The fence is my enemy.

Every time you look up at the stars, it's like opening a door. You could be anyone, anywhere. You could be yourself at any moment in your life. You open that door and you realize you're the same person under the same stars. Camping out in the backyard with your best friend, eleven years old. Sixteen, driving alone, stopping at the edge of the city, looking up at the same stars. Walking a wooded path, kissing in the moonlight, look up and you're eleven again. Chasing cats in a tiny town, you're eleven again, you're sixteen again. You're in a rowboat. You're staring out the back of a car. Out here where the world begins and ends, it's like nothing ever stops happening.

Have you seen a soul or any-thing?
Are you my sister?
Am I just...
...like, you know...
...totally crazy?

Hey, Raleigh, check it out.
Me and Dave caught three cats in this wicked box.
I maintain that the cats were in the box when they found it.
Remember how you can fuck off and die, Ferguson?
Z
BIG

Z
meow
meow
Hiss
grr
HISSS
SSSS
SNARL
myaa!
Um... can you maybe let them out or some-thing?
What are you, NUTS?
Well, I AM making you chase cats in the middle of the night.
meow?
meoww?
...
BIG

She IS making us chase cats in the middle of the night.
Suit yourself. It's all fun and games until someone loses an eye, right?
NYAAAAARGH
There they go.
How about that.
Woo! I got mine!

Hurry! It's overpowering me!
Eek! Sandpaper tongue!

Why am I here, chasing cats in the middle of the night? Why was I in California? Why is anything? The reason, the real reason, the primary secret sort of reason that I went to California, to Berkeley, is because Stillman wanted to meet me. Stillman, Stillman, Stillman. I put myself on a train, told my mother that I was visiting my father, took myself and my things across the horrible border and Washington and Oregon and into his arms.

And he was good. He was as good as such a thing ever could possibly be. He was good and right and everything was perfect and painless and I didn't stumble on words or lead conversations into painful dead ends. We made sandwiches and cooked pasta and kissed in the moonlight. The perfect guy turned out to be the perfect guy and we did everything and then I had to leave and—

This is totally the one with your soul, Raleigh.

No. No, but he knows something.
Okay, you're free to go.
Man, the humane society or whatever wouldn't like this one bit.

So I have a question.
Okay...?
What made you crazy?
BIG
TORONTO

You mean like how Magda made YOU crazy?
I've... I've kind of been trying to figure it out, actually.
See? It's a valid question, asshole.
TORONTO

I think this one is special.
I feel a specialness emanating from her.
Okay, Dave—
In grade three they took me out of class—
TORONTO

OW! Jesus!
In grade three...?
BIG
They told me I was gifted. They took me out of class.
They made a— a gifted class, we met once a week or something—
Hey, I was a gifted child.
TORONTO
BIG

Wh-
So was I.
TORONTO
You guys suck! I hate you! So I'm not fucking GIFTED.
Oh would you STOP.
TORONTO

In grade six, the start of middle school, they sent me to gifted class and for the first time I found out that in this wider world there were other actual gifted kids. Real ones, not the fake kind they had in my little elementary school. I found out that I wasn't alone and I wasn't special anymore and although maybe there were kids on my level, who I could maybe relate to, I was resentful. Age eleven and I was completely disillusioned. Age eighteen and nothing's changed.

For Aiur!!
Go! Go!
Fuck you guys. I'm sitting.
Oh, man. Yes.
I...
Hey... it's okay. Just relax.

No, there's...
I mean... wait.
I have
to—
I have
something
on my
chest.
TORONTO
...Oh.
Well, I
dunno how
I'll be
at—
Well, I mean,
I don't know.
But you should
say it, I
guess.

Like... well, say there was a girl, and a guy, and they started talking a lot.
On the internet, and later on the phone. And more and more.
And they talked about everything and it was really, like, the best talking that either of them'd ever had.

What if he was a couple years older, and in university, and American.
What if she was still in high school, and, and a year or so, maybe more—
—a year or so had passed since they started talking, and she was graduating. And he invited her to visit.
In California.
It could have been in California.

*ahem*

So what if she went to California and met him and everything went beautifully and she left to go home at the predetermined time, with her predetermined return ticket for the train, and he left her at the train station because he had to work, and she found this letter in her bag and she started crying like a baby because she just couldn't help it. And she missed her train. What if that?
What did the letter say?

I—she—
I—we didn't
open it.
I
couldn't
open it.
It was
too much. It's
unopened.
That's
like...
It's...it's
like carrying
a nuke around
in your bag,
man.

So... uh... what happened next...?
My phone rang.
TORONTO
Your ph—
My phone rang, and it was you.
Oh my god.

You guys were on some great end-of school self-discovery road trip thing, and I totally fucking crashed it.
And it was all-it-you called me by ACCIDENT. It was an ACCIDENT!

I ... I found my soul.
In one of the cats??
N-no, I mean... before. It's... I came here, to California, to get it back, I think?
TORONTO
And I did. I totally did. I got it back. I had it in my hand and I smiled this total Buddha smile.
And then he was gone, and all I had was this letter and the emptiness again.
And then I was in a car with you guys. And I'm a total shit, aren't I?

I'm an anti-social monster. I'm such a fuckup. I'm — I'm — I'm a mediocre fuckup, even. I'm not even good at fucking up!!!
He might not love me?? That's cause for a fucking breakdown?! What is this?? I'm stupid! I feel stupid! I'm horrible!!
No... no. I mean, no. It's — it's all-valid.
You're allowed to feel fucked up. You're not horrible. You're amazing. You dazzle.
I mean, you just made frie with us in two days. Look at you You're our new best friend.
You're MY new best friend.

I haven't had a best friend since grade 8.
Four years, six months... um...
Grade 6 for me.
All the girls in high school seemed, like... I dunno. Useless?
TORONTO
But you... I always thought you were so fucking cool, Raleigh.
Are— are you serious?
If so, you were so, so, so amazingly wrong.

I was not wrong. Not even. You're so cool. You're like the coolest person ever.
And any-way, I know you're all fucked up or whatever, but, I mean, so am I, okay?
So's everyone. Or everyone I know, anyway.
Look at Dave and Ian!
Dave seems... um, kind of nor-mal, in a way...
Dave is so fucked up! Don't even get me star-ted on that guy.
TORONTO

But you guys— you—you seem to have it all figured out. You know? You DEAL.
As if you don't? What do you call this shit?
Look at you— god, half an hour past your life's great trauma and you're stuck in a car with three crazy assholes you hardly know?
You're dealing with a lot.
A LOT.

I'd be dead if I was you.
I'm... I'm dead. I think I'm dead. Seriously.
TORONTO
You're not dead. Shut up. Look at you. You're alive. You're fucking hardcore.

You're-
Fuck... I don't know.

I guess I never have any answers. Just the same pointless question, over and over, every day: why am I so fucked up why am I so fucked up why am I so fucked up why am I so fucked up. Maybe that's just mental. Maybe I should stop. Maybe I already have. Maybe it's important to open up to people—people who are right there with you, not some thousand miles away in another universe. Or maybe it's something else. Maybe I should just settle for not knowing. Maybe it's good just to know that you're not the only one who doesn't know. Maybe... maybe I should stop thinking. Maybe I'll shut the fuck up.

I don't understand exactly what's happened, and I'm bad at putting things together in any meaningful way, but tonight is important— this moment is important.

The rest of the story is that they fixed the car and we got back on the road and we talked and we laughed and we went places and probably eventually got home. And after that, every time we saw a cat, it was a thing, and there were so many other things, and having in-jokes was nice. Generally the rest of the story was probably more interesting if you were there and the jokes probably seemed funnier at the time.

And I babbled. I stumbled over words. I wondered if they secretly hated me. I wasn't always happy, and it was a long time before I stopped feeling that fee[illegible] of you behind me, around me, inside me, you, [illegible] m[illegible]tillman — the feeling of us. And I wasn't always happy, but I think I was generally getting better, and if I had no soul, well, maybe I just stopped worrying about it. ...Eventually.

onto it, it will maybe never end, the way it feels like my time with you never ended, the way it's still going on in the background. I l[illegible]e the tops o[illegible]trees, and I love the sound o[illegible]eff Tweedy's voice, and I love the hiss of the wheels on the pavement behind it all going a million miles an hour in the deep dark lovely middle of the night.

And I will wonder forever if I'll see you again, or for six days, or for eight months, or for five years, or for the rest of my horrible, beautiful life. And other things will happen to me that are just as amazing and lovely and traumatizing as you have been, and I will tell you none of them. Maybe. And sometimes I try to stop speculating the future out of existence, and other times I just lean back and run with it because maybe it's for the best.

I am leaning back and running with it and staring at the stars and I'm eleven, I'm sixteen, I'm eighteen, I'm a newborn, I'm everyone everywhere with you without you unbound set free in limbo lost at sea.

Bryan Lee O'Malley was born and raised in Canada. He has been making comics since an early age. When he drew this one, he was 24 years old. He has an extremely great website at WWW.RADIOMARU.COM.

**ILLUSTRATION** *of the* **AUTHOR**
*by* **NATHAN AVERY**

# OTHER BOOKS FROM BRYAN LEE O'MALL

**SCOTT PILGRIM, VOLUME 1:**
**SCOTT PILGRIM'S PRECIOUS LITTLE L**
By Bryan Lee O'Malley
168 pages, digest, B&W
$11.99
ISBN 978-1-932664-08-9

---

**SCOTT PILGRIM, VOLUME 2:**
**SCOTT PILGRIM VS. THE WORLD**
By Bryan Lee O'Malley
200 pages, digest, B&W
$11.99 US
ISBN 978-1-932664-12-6

---

**SCOTT PILGRIM, VOLUME 3:**
**SCOTT PILGRIM & THE INFINITE SADN**
By Bryan Lee O'Malley
184 pages, digest, B&W
$11.99 US
ISBN 978-1-932664-22-5

---

**SCOTT PILGRIM, VOLUME 4:**
**SCOTT PILGRIM GETS IT TOGETHER**
By Bryan Lee O'Malley
216 pages, digest, B&W
$11.99 US
ISBN 978-1-932664-49-2

---

**SCOTT PILGRIM, VOLUME 5:**
**SCOTT PILGRIM VS. THE UNIVERSE**
By Bryan Lee O'Malley
184 pages, digest, B&W
$11.99
ISBN 978-1-934964-10-1

---

**SCOTT PILGRIM, VOLUME 6:**
**SCOTT PILGRIM'S FINEST HOUR**
By Bryan Lee O'Malley
248 pages, digest, B&W
$11.99
ISBN 978-1-934964-38-5

www.onipress.com | www.scottpilgrim.com

For more information on these and other fine Oni Press comic books and graphic novels, visit www.onipress.co
To find a comic specialty store in your area, call 1-888-COMICBOOK or visit www.comicshops.us.